OPERATION TIGER

G. L. EAVES

iUniverse, Inc.
Bloomington

Operation Tiger

iUniverse books may be ordered through booksellers or by contacting:

iUniverse
1663 Liberty Drive
Bloomington, IN 47403
www.iuniverse.com
1-800-Authors (1-800-288-4677)

Because of the dynamic nature of the Internet, any web addresses or links contained in this book may have changed since publication and may no longer be valid. The views expressed in this work are solely those of the author and do not necessarily reflect the views of the publisher, and the publisher hereby disclaims any responsibility for them.

Any people depicted in stock imagery provided by Thinkstock are models, and such images are being used for illustrative purposes only.

Certain stock imagery © Thinkstock.

ISBN: 978-1-4620-1274-9 (sc)
ISBN: 978-1-4620-1276-3 (hc)
ISBN: 978-1-4620-1275-6 (ebk)

Library of Congress Control Number: 2011905642

Printed in the United States of America

iUniverse rev. date: 11/13/2011

Dedicated with love
to my son, Matt, and my daughter, Cydney

Contents

1. The Best Day of My Life 1

2. Zingers, Anyone? 5

3. The Secret Weapon 11

4. All Gooped Up 19

5. Stalking the Wild Babe 25

6. Love 'Em and Leave 'Em.................33

7. Scoot a Boot 37

8. A Fool for Love 43

9. Golden Moldies 49

10. Dare to Dial...................55

11. Have a Nice Trip 59

12. Cover Me................63

13. Just Say It.................69

14. Out on a Limb.................73

15. Project Cookie 79

16. Cookie Intercepted 85

17. Chicken Dance 89

18. The Tiger Purrs 93

Acknowledgments

I offer heartfelt appreciation to my family and the many students I have known over the years who provided inspiration for these characters and this story.

I am also very thankful to Laura Chong, who created the original cover illustration.

Chapter 1

The Best Day of My Life

My name is Aaron Wesley Haberman. I know I've said it before, but this day really *was* the best day of my life. My sixth-grade teacher, Ms. Newhouse, assigned students a group project on the history of Halloween. Now, I like putting on fangs and fake blood as much as the next person, but I think we've done this project every year since the second grade. It wasn't the report I was excited about.

It was embarrassing enough to still be in elementary school, the last sixth-grade class to be there. After this year, all sixth graders would go to middle school. But here we were, with the little kids, doing Halloween reports yet again.

What changed my life was that there were six kids to each Halloween group and Kristin Kramer was in mine. She is, well, really cute. Her blonde hair is way past her shoulders and reminds me of a shampoo commercial. Her eyes are more gray than blue. This was the chance I'd been waiting for.

I have known Kristin since fourth grade. She happens to be

pretty, smart, nice, and athletic. I guess you could say I have loved her from afar. We have never been in the same class until this year, so I get to see her every day. I'm not usually shy, but I never can get up the nerve to approach her. She says "Hi" or "Hi, Aaron" and that's about it. Then I can never think of anything to say. I just stand there, trying to remember to breathe.

I figured this was pretty ridiculous since I was almost twelve years old. Why was I so afraid? So freaked out? I decided there must be a way to get over this. So I'd been trying to come up with a plan to get her to notice me, like me, go out with me someday. I mean, I'm not bad. On the good side, I'm pretty tall, smart, and have really muscular legs. On the bad side, I'm smart, wear glasses, and am polite to teachers. (These are bad, at least according to Kyle Landers, who *is* the definition of cool.)

Right after lunch, we moved into our groups and formed a circle. Phil Tolbert, my neighbor and friend, ended up sitting between Kristin and Jessica Norton, who is pretty cute too. I was between Larry Shumberg and Alicia Brown. I was not a happy camper.

Phil had the seat of honor in this group, and I didn't think he deserved it. I was beginning to have ideas of torture for dear Phil that involved a rack, a spiked stick, and dripping, gray dungeon walls. I may be shy around one specific girl, but there is nothing wrong with my imagination.

However, as I was sitting across the circle from Kristin, I did get to admire her. She even has great ankles. She seems so delicate, but you should see her play soccer. I started daydreaming about being on the opposing team during a game. *Kristin is in control of the ball, and I am the goalie. She's going to kick the ball any second. Should I dive and block it, or let her score? Here she comes!*

"Your outlines are due tomorrow, so get busy. Remember, you may want to choose a recorder in your group so ... blah, blah, blah," Ms. Newhouse rambled on. I drifted back to the imaginary soccer game.

"I'll be the recorder," Jessica said.

Jessica is always willing to write anything. She believes she has the best handwriting in the world, and she's probably right. When she isn't writing, she has always had this annoying habit of twirling her pen in her short red hair. It's really weird. She may look okay, but this pen thing bugs me.

"If you want to, we can all get together at my house after school," Kristin suggested. "I know some great websites and we can print out all the notes we need."

I would have swallowed my gum if I had been chewing any. I would actually be able to go to her house! This was too good to be true. That's when I knew it would definitely be the best day of my life. Okay, at least the best day this week.

Chapter 2

Zingers, Anyone?

For the rest of the day, I admit, I did a lot of daydreaming. I'm pretty bad about that, according to my teachers and parents. But I find that daydreaming is a very practical way to spend time. It lets me work out solutions to all kinds of problems and situations. This time, I needed to be prepared about how I was going to act when I got to Kristin's house. I was nervous and excited at the same time.

I couldn't figure out if I should act irritated, like I was so busy after school that it was tough to find time to drop by her house. Or if I should act real serious, like this assignment was important because I naturally wanted to do a good job and get a good grade. Maybe I should just goof around a lot and try to make her laugh. It would be a great opportunity without a teacher breathing down my neck. It seemed like the goofing-around plan was probably the best.

When the last bell rang, I ran outside. It was gray and drizzly and a little cold, so my mom would be picking me up. She insists on doing that, but I don't really care. It doesn't bother me to walk home in lousy weather. As soon as I saw our van, I hurried and jumped in.

"Mom, quick, take me home so I can change my shirt. No! Never mind. Oh, great, you brought me a giant grape Sloshee. Do you have a hairbrush in your purse?"

"Slow down," Mom said as she pulled out into the slow-moving traffic. "What's going on? You look a little frantic."

"Our group is meeting at Kristin's house. Can you believe it?" I had already polished off almost half of my purple drink.

"Do you know where she lives?" Mom asked.

"Eleven twenty-five Willow, right around the corner from the Martins," I said.

"Oh, that's right, you said Kristin's house. I should have guessed that you would know." Mom smiled. "Are you nervous?" She usually has me figured out pretty well. But that's only because I choose to tell her stuff. She's pretty cool most of the time, except when she gets mad and acts like a mother. So we talk a lot more than some kids and their moms do.

"No. Yeah. I don't know. I just don't want to do anything stupid right there in her house."

"Just be yourself—you're a sharp guy. She'll notice if you just don't try so hard."

"Mom, I'm not sharp, I'm a *geek*." Uh-oh, I knew I shouldn't have said that. It always starts off a long speech where she tells me how great I am and I don't have to be like everyone else and just wait until I'm grown and successful.

"You are not ..." she started.

"Mom, please, we have to hurry … I'll try to be myself. I need that brush."

We were close to Kristin's house, and at a stop sign, Mom reached into the suitcase she calls a purse and handed me a small pink brush. I slid down in the seat so no one could see me using it. When I finished, I pulled down the sun visor and looked into the mirror to check my hair.

"AAAhhhh!" I yelled, making Mom swerve the car a little. "My mouth is purple!" My lips, tongue, and teeth were stained a dark purple from the Sloshee. I couldn't go in like this!

"Mom, drive around the block. I look like I've been sucking on a purple marker!"

Mom looked over at me and started to tell me it wasn't so bad. Instead, she frowned and said, "Here, drink some of my water. Maybe it will fade." She always carries water with her because drinking a lot of it is supposed to help her lose weight. Right now, I was really glad she wasn't skinny.

I drank the water and rubbed my mouth and teeth with the inside of my shirt. It didn't help much. "This is the worst day of my life," I groaned.

Mom tried to think of something, searching again in her purse. She offered me gum, lip gloss (sure!), and hand lotion to rub on my lips.

In the end, I knew I had two choices: I could skip the meeting and miss my only chance to be in Kristin's house. Or I could go anyway, purple mouth and all. I imagined trying to go in and laugh it off. I sort of drifted into another daydream.

"Mom! Can you drive me back to the Food Mart?"

She didn't look pleased. "Aaron, I need to pick up your sister at Kim's house," she said, looking at her watch.

"Mom, please? This is an emergency. I have a plan."

"Well, I'm glad someone does. I'll do it if you hurry. Do you have money?" she asked.

I felt in my jeans pocket. I had some change left from lunch. I hoped it would be enough and nodded, giving her my best purple smile.

Running into the convenience store, I quickly grabbed a handful of candy and paid the clerk. I even had a nickel left.

"Well?" asked Mom as I got back into the car.

"Mouth Zingers."

"Mouth Zingers?" Mom didn't exactly keep up with candy and other good junk.

"Bite into one of these babies and your mouth is stained an awesome color. Should last at least until the meeting is over." I was feeling pretty hopeful about this plan. Except I still had to walk in and get laughed at before I could pass the candy around.

Just as we pulled up at Kristin's house, I saw Phil ringing her doorbell. I jumped out of the car. "Phil! Wait!" I raced up to him and shoved the candy into his hand. "I'm providing treats. Be sure and hand them out as soon as you go in. I'll be right back."

Phil had already unwrapped a blue Zinger and was chomping away. His mouth and teeth were bright blue. I walked slowly back to the car to tell Mom I would just walk home. I stayed at the car window, trying to keep her there so I would have an excuse to go in after everyone had been "zinged." She finally drove away, telling me to go in and get it over with.

Walking in slow motion, I made it up the sidewalk, up the steps, and to the door. I slowly reached up and rang the doorbell. I heard a lot of laughing inside.

Kristin's toothy red grin greeted me. "Hi, Aaron, come in. Ooh, you're purple," she said, laughing.

"This is gross candy," said Alicia Brown, with frowning orange lips.

"I like it!" Larry Shumberg said. He had chosen a black Zinger and now looked like a zombie or something. Larry didn't look that great even with his regular face.

Jessica looked up and saw me, and quickly covered her green mouth with her hand.

"Good job, Phil," I whispered as I walked past him and sat down.

"We better get to work, guys," said Kristin, not the least bit bothered by her red-stained mouth.

I thought she looked beautiful and probably would have with almost any color teeth.

Chapter 3

The Secret Weapon

When I woke up the morning after the meeting at Kristin's, I felt a little depressed, like I didn't have that much to look forward to. These kinds of feelings usually last only a few minutes, until I get busy and forget about them, but I really hate feeling that way.

"What's wrong, Aaron?" Mom could tell from the look on my face.

"Nothing." Almost any kid will automatically give this answer, and it almost never works.

"Did something happen at school yesterday?" Mom tried to sound casual while she stirred oatmeal for my little sister, Sarah.

"No, Mom."

"Well, if you want to talk about it, just ..."

"Mom, I don't know, okay?"

"Okay, okay ... Sarah, don't pour your juice into the oatmeal, please."

"But I'm the cooking girl." Sarah was only four. Sometimes

she talked like she was two and sometimes she sounded about eight.

"Oh, how was the meeting at Kristin's house?" Mom asked. "I forgot to ask you if your plan worked."

I got a little dreamy eyed. "It worked perfectly! Everyone's teeth were awesome colors. And Kristin was beau—uh, really cool about it."

I saw Mom smiling as she finished packing our lunches. Man, I hoped I hadn't said too much. But then, she knew I liked Kristin. She was no dummy.

"Do you have a girlfriend, Aaron?" my nosy sister asked in an annoying singsong voice. What did she know about girlfriends and boyfriends and stuff?

"You watch too much TV," I told her. "We're friends, you know? That's all. We just like to hang out and talk." Now, that was funny. The only long conversation we had had was about where Halloween came from and why there were costumes for witches and vampires. Still, it had been fun just to talk to her about anything.

My dumb, nosy little sister wasn't even listening. She was playing with the last of her stupid oatmeal.

"Aaron, if you're planning on going trick-or-treating tomorrow night, you better plan a costume. Don't wait until the last minute. Well, I guess it already is the last minute."

"I thought I'd go as an android. You know, half human and half robot," I said.

"Well, I think we have plenty of makeup for that. Who else is going?" Mom asked.

"Phil and Chris." I was lucky to have two friends on my street. Chris was in another class and his parents made him do a lot of chores, so I was glad to have a chance to see him.

"You know Dad thinks you're too old to go trick-or-treating," Mom said.

"Like I would pass up a chance for all that free candy?" I couldn't believe how bizarre parents could be sometimes, especially my dad.

"It *is* more for the little kids, Aaron. I always think it's ridiculous for kids as tall as I am to come to the door with pillowcases, ready to load up on junk." Mom gave me that look over her shoulder. The look that meant, "You know I'm right."

"Well, this will probably be the last year I go," I said. I had also said that for the last two years.

"Brush your teeth, kids, it's time for school. Hurry!" Mom was shifting into fast gear to get everybody out the door on time. Dad leaves early, so it's just the three of us most mornings. I was glad he hadn't overheard the Halloween discussion. It was much simpler that way.

"I'm not in school, Mom, I'm in PREschool," Sarah said.

"Yes, preschool. Get your jackets and backpacks."

"OK, Mom." I brushed my teeth and took a last look at my hair. Mom says I have good hair, but I hate it. It's dark brown and thick and won't lie down like everyone else's. She always says the girls will love it. I keep trying to tell her they don't. I went out the door with my hair dripping wet and slicked down, but as soon as it dried, it puffed back up again.

When I got to school, I decided to try again to think of something to talk to Kristin about.

Then maybe the day wouldn't be a total loss. Maybe she was going out on Halloween too. She lived only a few blocks away. That would be so cool if we ran into each other.

I usually have to stay in my own neighborhood. This bothers my mom almost as much as it bothers me. Halloween is her favorite holiday, and she always talks about how sorry she is that things have changed and that now it's dangerous to go out and wander very far.

She or my dad always goes with my sister, and I go with friends. Some little kids go to the mall, but that's just not the same. So after we make the rounds, we pour candy on the floor, and I help my parents check all the pieces before they go into the "safe" pile. I eat the suspicious ones, just to protect my little sister, of course.

I saw Kristin coming into the classroom and managed to step in right behind her.

"Hey, Kristin. Are you going out tomorrow night?" Right after I said it, I hoped she knew I meant trick-or-treating, and not *going out*, like on a date.

"Yeah, I think so," she answered.

And then, I couldn't think of anything else to say. I just stood there and blanked out. This is what always happens. I needed to have a conversation plan. I needed to know what to say after she said something. I needed help.

Later, at lunch, I went over to Kyle Landers's table. There is something about Kyle, something every guy wishes for. He's real good at sports, makes decent grades, has about a million friends, and has girls calling him at home. I don't know how he does it. But I knew that if anyone could help me, he could.

"Hey, Kyle," I said.

"Hey-hey-Haber-MAN," Kyle said, laughing. He always calls me that. Like he's stuttering. At first I thought he was making fun of my last name, Haberman, but now I think he's just having fun, because he gets this goofy look on his face when he does it. Like he's having some problem talking. If someone else did this, that person would be weird, but when Kyle does it, it's funny. When the kid next to Kyle got up, I sat down next to him.

"I need to talk to you about something," I said in a low voice.

"Is eet about ze secret veapon?" Kyle whispered in a mixed-up accent.

"Yeah, I need one." I tried to lift one eyebrow, to look mysterious and play along.

"Ah, come vith me to the laBORatory and ve shall see vhat ve can do," Kyle said, looking back and forth across the lunchroom, as if spies were everywhere.

"No, meet me after school, Agent Landers, and you can give me the weapon then," I said, slipping away from the table and edging my way along the cafeteria wall. Kyle was watching me and laughing.

Kyle and I were kind of friends, I guess. But I am always a little surprised when he acts friendly with me in public.

At the end of the day, I hung around Kyle's class until he came out.

"What's up, hey-hey-Haber-MAN?"

"Come outside." I led him out by the bike racks. It was a nice day, so I would be walking home and had some time to pick his brain.

"I need some ideas for, you know, getting a … babe," I said.

"Ideas?"

"Like how to talk to her, ask her out, that kind of stuff."

"No problem, dude," Kyle said, smiling. "Is she in your class?"

"Maybe," I answered, not feeling like telling him who I was after.

"Ah, the mystery babe. She won't talk to you?"

"Not much. She's friendly, but …"

"What do you mean, she's friendly?" Kyle asked.

"Well, she smiles when we talk, but she just doesn't say much, and I can't ever think of anything past one line … 'Hi, whatcha doing?' … 'Not much' … This kind of meaningful conversation," I said.

"Have you ever caught her looking at you?" Kyle asked.

"Maybe." I tried to remember. "The other day when my mouth was purple, she looked at me a lot."

"I'm not sure that counts," Kyle said. "But for now, let's say she likes you. As far as you know, you've got a chance with her. You have to figure out a way to be with her, and talk to her, without her friends around."

"Why?" I asked.

Kyle looked at me like I was crazy. "Because if her friends are around, she'll act totally different. She won't be interested in anything except acting like she's not embarrassed about you talking to her. She won't even listen to you."

"Dr. Love Landers, you have all the inside information, I guess," I said, laughing.

"Well, that's why you came to the best." Kyle grinned. "Remember, Haber-MAN, I have an older sister. I have women figured out."

I just looked at him. "My dad says that's impossible."

Chapter 4

All Gooped Up

On Halloween night, my mom always makes us eat vegetable soup and whole-wheat bread for dinner. I guess she feels like that is healthy enough to make up for all the junk we will have the rest of the night. At least she isn't pushing liver and broccoli.

I was trying to artfully smear white makeup over my face so I could look like an android. My dad had actually found a space-captain uniform shirt at a costume shop near his office. Just when I think he's going to drive me crazy being strict and stuff, he goes and does something nice like that.

"Aaron's making a mess," sang my tattling little sister.

"Shut up, Sarah," I said, trying not to move my lips very much because of all the goop I had on them.

"Mom!" Sarah wailed. "He said 'shut up'!" To be so short, she sure had a loud voice.

"That's right, rat face. Shut up."

She punched me in the stomach and ran. She does that a lot.

Such a charming little kid. And I was too busy to chase her at the moment.

"Aaron, perhaps you've forgotten our agreement to stop saying inappropriate things to your sister," Mom said a little sarcastically as she came in my room. "Oh, gosh, what a mess."

"Sorry, Mom. This stuff is messy." I tried to look pitiful and held up my hands, all smeared with white makeup. Everything I had touched in the room had white smudges on it. I didn't remember touching that many things, but I guess I had. Mom was already trying to wipe things down with the dish towel she had carried in.

"You missed a spot," she said, and began blending something on my cheek so I wouldn't have pink spots of skin showing.

"Should I do my eyebrows?" I asked.

"Do everything, I think," she said, trying to remember exactly what androids looked like. "You look like you definitely need some sun. There, that looks better. Now you need to slick your hair back." She brought me some superstrong hair gel, which I wasn't sure would work.

I had decided to make candy second on my list that night. I was mainly going to concentrate on trying to run into Kristin and her friends as they went door-to-door. It would help if I knew what costume she would be wearing, but I hadn't been brave enough to ask her.

Sarah and Mom and Dad checked on me right before they went out. Sarah was dressed like some kind of bee or something. They should have rigged up some kind of stinger for her rear end, but she had only these dumb little wings, some fake antennae, and a striped shirt.

"Stay with the group, Aaron, and remember to stay in the neighborhood. I still can't believe you're doing this. At your age," said Dad, shaking his head.

"Be careful. Don't trip over anything. Watch out for cars and be home by about nine," Mom said. They always said the same things on Halloween. I had been through this so many times. I guess it made them feel better to say it again this year.

"Don't forget to say 'trick or treat' and 'thank you,'" Sarah lectured. Like I really needed advice from a bee.

I grabbed an old pillowcase and threw in a few pairs of socks so that if I didn't get much candy, no one would be able to tell. I was supposed to meet Phil and Chris on the corner.

"You already got some candy?" asked Phil, spying my pillowcase as I walked up. He was dressed like a hippie in some old clothes of his parents. Tie-dyed shirt, headband, old wig with long hair, and bell-bottom pants. He was even carrying a plastic flower and giving the old peace sign with his other hand. He had a button on his shirt that said "Flower Power."

"Uh, yeah, a little," I said. "Nice outfit, Phil. Oh man, Chris—your hair, dude!"

Chris was going as a rapper. His mother had made him some dreadlocks out of black yarn and sort of weaved them into his own hair. It was hilarious. He was bouncing either to some music in his head or to a player hooked up that I couldn't see.

"Yo, hey, robot-man, you're looking real good ..." he said.

"Where are we going first? Let's do Birchfield and then come back in this direction," suggested Phil.

"I have a different idea, and I need your help," I said as we started walking. "I need you guys to help me watch for Kristin. We need to start on her street."

"Man, are you crazy? I don't wanna go that far. That's wasting time," Chris said, very concerned about his empty loot bag.

"Oh, Kristin! You like her, Aaron?" Phil asked. Like he was just discovering this. Sometimes it takes Phil a little while to catch on.

"Let's just go. Her street is supposed to have a couple of houses that really load you up." I was making up that part, but it worked. We walked as fast as we could, Phil and Chris suddenly agreeable.

I checked out every group of girls we passed, but none of them looked like they could be Kristin. Once I thought I heard her laughing, but it was Alicia Brown, dressed up like a cheerleader.

Our candy collection wasn't going very well, either. Several adults looked irritated to find us at the door. They were all smiles for the little kids. We were just bigger little kids who still loved candy. Is that so wrong? We were polite, so I don't think anyone was really mad. Except maybe this one old guy who gave us a dirty look and threw *one* tiny piece of candy into each of our bags. Made us wish we weren't too nice to soap his windows or pour syrup on his front porch.

We were about to head back toward our part of the neighborhood when I spotted a different group coming up the sidewalk on the other side of the street. Only one of them had blonde hair. It was dark, but I figured it had to be her, gorgeous in a red, glittery dance costume.

I was feeling pretty brave, as I always do when I am in a disguise. I circled back and got behind them. I got as close as I could to Kristin and put my hands on her waist. "Trick or treat!" I said in my emotionless android voice. She gasped and turned around.

It wasn't Kristin. It was a girl in the seventh grade. I barely remembered seeing her at school last year. "Excuse me?" she asked in a real nasty voice. Like I was some slug contaminating her with my slime.

"Uh, sorry. Thought you were someone else." I knew my face was blood red under the white makeup. I turned to run back across the street and bumped right into a masked Darth Vader, the main *Star Wars* bad guy.

"You dare to cross my path?" Darth said in a husky whisper. The black visor went up and it was Kristin, laughing wildly. "You had the funniest look on your face, Aaron," she said.

"I ... uh ... excuse me, Kristin," I stammered. "I thought ... I didn't ... Never mind."

"You look great! Have you gotten much candy?" she asked.

"Tons. Looks like it's gonna be a great night," I lied. "How about you?"

"Not really. No one is giving us much. Maybe we're too old. Well, see ya." She waved and pulled her visor down again. Making the famous heavy breathing sounds, she walked off to join her friends.

Chapter 5

Stalking the Wild Babe

It was no big surprise that I woke up the morning after Halloween feeling embarrassed. Androids may not have emotions, but I sure did. Not even the decent load of candy I collected could make me feel better. Every time I was around Kristin, I messed up. I was getting sick of it. She must have thought of me as the supreme jerk of all time.

At the breakfast table, I glanced at the front page of the newspaper, imagining a headline that read "Local Sixth Grader Named Top Geek in State Competition." It would feature a fuzzy photograph of me with my hair even puffier than usual and in some stupid striped shirt that was a size too small.

I thought about what Kyle had said, but following his advice was not going to be all I needed. Kristin was always around her friends, and I didn't figure I could exactly make them disappear just so I could speak to Kristin privately. Girls in our school traveled in packs. Catching one alone was as hard as playing a video game without using your thumbs.

That morning, our teacher showed a nature video, and I even managed to watch part of it. It was all about these tigers in India and how they stalk their prey. They played it calm and cool, confidently watching their target and then pouncing when the time was right.

I had a little mini-brainstorm. I would learn from the master hunter and develop a plan. I would launch "Operation Tiger." It would allow me to close in on Kristin without bumbling or running into a wall or anything. She wouldn't really be my prey, but at least a plan to "catch her" would help.

I had watched Kristin from a distance for a long time. I made some mental notes on her schedule. She always went straight to the water fountain at the end of the day before walking home with Jessica. She rode with Jessica's mother if the weather was bad. She sat with Jessica at lunch. I began to see a pattern here.

Perhaps Jessica could be useful. If I could persuade her to be my accomplice, that would be all I needed. If Jessica put in a good word for me, surely Kristin would listen. Why shouldn't she? Now I just had to figure out how to get Jessica's attention and talk her into giving me a little inside information.

At PE, Phil came up to me, sweaty and breathing hard after a fierce round of basketball drills. I loved basketball and could play all afternoon without getting very winded.

"Aaron, did you hear about Chris?" Phil wiped sweat off his forehead with his sleeve.

"No, what?" I asked.

"His cousin got a record contract."

"The one in that rap group? From LA or somewhere?" I

couldn't believe it. I was best friends with someone who now had a famous cousin. Thoughts of being invited up on stage developed quickly. *The applause is shattering. A member of the stage crew asks me to come up and jam with the newest hip-hop bad boys. Kristin asks for my autograph, and so does everyone else.*

"It's probably not even true." Phil managed to burst my pleasant little daydream.

"Chris doesn't lie, Phil. This could be my big break." I started to slip into my stage fantasy again. *I am in a silver limo and girls press their noses to the window. They are screaming my name, and a couple are smiling and crying at the same time.*

A shrill whistle made my eardrums tingle. "Boys! Line up for class. Now!" Coach boomed across the gym.

The day dragged on like a bad movie, but finally the last bell rang. Everyone scooped up their books and broke for the door, eager for the freedom of the outside world.

"Kristin, can I speak with you a moment?" Ms. Newhouse called.

This was my chance with Jessica. I hurried outside and posted myself by the door, ready to talk to her alone while I had the chance. Funny, this wasn't nearly as tough as trying to talk to Kristin.

"Pssst, Jessica. Come here," I whispered a little frantically.

"What's up, Aaron?" She came over to where I was. She stood real close to me, smiling like I was giving away free video-arcade passes or something.

"Uh …" Maybe I wasn't prepared enough for this. "I need you to, you know, talk to Kristin for me," I blundered.

"What about?" Jessica frowned a little.

I looked quickly back at the classroom door, sure Kristin would walk out any minute. "Ask her if she … Ask her who she likes."

"Why, Aaron? Do you like her? Oh, you *do*. I figured." Jessica suddenly looked bored.

"Just do me that favor, okay, Jess?" I hoped calling her "Jess" would make her feel like we were buddies. You know, anything for a friend and all that. "Can I call you tonight?"

"I guess so. My dad doesn't like it very much, but he doesn't get home until seven," she said.

Kristin came out with her backpack hanging on one shoulder. I felt my face get hot and wished that it was physically possible for me to kick myself. "Hi, Kristin," I managed to say.

"Did you get a lot of candy last night?" Kristin asked.

"Yeah. How about you?"

"We finally did! I weighed it," she said. "The bag was ten pounds! Do you realize how much that would cost if you bought it at the mall shop? My parents were freaking out."

I laughed. I usually weighed mine too, but I had been too bummed to do it last night.

"See ya tomorrow." Kristin turned and started talking to Jessica as they walked off.

"See ya," I called after them. I just couldn't figure her out. She was always nice to everyone. If she liked someone, I didn't know who it was. Maybe Jessica did.

I stopped by Chris's house on the way home to find out more about the rap group news, but he wasn't home. Maybe I would be the group's local publicity manager. I needed some fame and respect, any way I could get it.

My sister had her paper and crayons all over the kitchen table where I usually drop my notebooks, so I hurried to the little desk in my room and raced through my homework.

"Aaron, look at my picture," Sarah said, bringing in a large piece of manila paper with a sun, a house, some birds, and a girl and a boy kissing, drawn neatly in waxy colors. She always drew a variation of the same thing.

"This is Michael and me," she said, grinning. She had liked him for a year. I guess long crushes run in the family.

"Hi, baby," Mom said to me as she passed by my room with a load of laundry. "How much homework do you have?" She asked this every day.

I usually say, "Not much." Sometimes I say, "I finished it at school." Today I said, "I'm almost done."

"I need you to put away your laundry when you're finished," she said as she disappeared down the hall. "The last load of your clothes is drying now."

I hated chores, even though I didn't have to do as many as Chris did. He and his brothers worked for three hours every Saturday morning. Their house must be really clean if their whole family works that long. My mom said they probably vacuum the drapes and polish the kitchen cabinet doors every week. Sometimes I think she hates house chores as much as I do. I wish she loved it, so I wouldn't have to help.

I finished the last math problem, shoved my clean underwear and socks into drawers and ran to grab the portable phone, but the battery wasn't charged, so I had to use the old phone with the long stretched out coiled cord.

"Hello, may I please speak to Jessica?" I had pretty smooth phone manners. Her mother seemed slightly impressed.

"Hello, Aaron," Jessica answered.

"How did you know?" I asked.

"Duh. Caller ID," she explained.

"Oh yeah." I rolled my eyes at myself. "Listen, Jess, did you talk to Kristin? Does she like anyone?" I was nervous about the answers I might get, so I was twisting the phone cord around my fingers as I talked.

"She … does … like someone," Jessica said, dragging it out and driving me crazy.

"Well?" I asked. "Come on, tell me!"

"She likes … Kyle," she said.

I felt my stomach turn inside out and back again. No way. I mean, every girl liked Kyle, but Kristin was supposed to be, well, different.

"Aaron? You okay?" Jessica asked. "It's no big deal, you know."

"Yeah, no big deal. Except that I might puke," I said, talking more to myself than to her.

"Oh, Aaron, don't be upset. Maybe, uh, maybe she won't like him very long." Jessica seemed to be trying to cheer me up.

"How long has she liked him?" I asked miserably. I noticed the tips of two fingers were turning reddish purple. I unwound the tight phone cord from my hand and moved my fingers to see if they still worked. Not that I would need them to punch in Kristin's phone number or anything.

"I don't know. Maybe you should try to make her jealous," Jessica suggested.

"How could I make her jealous if she doesn't even like me?" I was confused.

"Well, I mean, maybe it would get her attention if she thought you liked someone else," she said.

"I think *we* should get another plan," I said. Maybe if Jessica thought she was part of a team effort here, she would come up with a better idea.

"Okay, then maybe you could try to show her you like the same things she likes," Jessica said.

This sounded much more logical to me. I didn't want to get into a "make someone jealous" game. That was for pros, and I was definitely an amateur.

"I'll vote for that. Commence Operation Tiger." I felt better already.

"What's Operation Tiger?" she asked.

"Never mind, Jessica. Ask her about everything she likes and tell me tomorrow." I was getting dirty looks from my dad. He was home early and obviously needed to use the phone.

We hung up and I felt hopeful in spite of what Jessica had said about Kyle. I happened to know that Kyle changed girlfriends about twice a month. But just in case, I thought I might walk over to his house and have a little chat.

"Where are you going?" Dad asked.

"Over to Kyle's for a few minutes," I said, slipping out before he could ask me more.

Chapter 6

Love 'Em and Leave 'Em

As usual, Kyle was outside shooting baskets. He had just gotten home from soccer practice. He was the most athletic guy in school. He was planning to be a professional sports figure and rake in the cash. After that he would be a celebrity sportscaster, just for fun. He had it all figured out. All I knew about my future was that I didn't want to have to get up very early for whatever job I ended up doing.

Without saying anything, I grabbed the ball on a high bounce and tried a jump shot from about fifteen feet out. I missed. It wasn't surprising, since I had other things on my mind. We played for a while, Kyle's agility impressing me all over again. Playing with him did improve my skills, though. He moved like a bionic cat, all grace and power. He was always grinning when he played. I would grin too if I were that good.

"Who you going out with now, Kyle?" I asked casually as we took turns drinking from a large jug of cold water his mom had brought out.

"Angela," he said, raising his eyebrows up and down really fast.

"No one else?" I asked. "I thought love 'em and leave 'em was your motto."

"There are a lot of beautiful women out there, Aaron. I just do the best I can. Why do you ask?" He poured the last few drops of water on top of his head and shook out his curly black hair.

"Just wondered. I was talking to Jessica and …"

"Jessica! Now, she's pretty hot." He glared at me with his pale blue eyes. "You like her?"

"Nah. I mean, only as a friend." I dribbled the ball as we stood there.

"So who is this mystery babe you were going to hit on?" Kyle asked.

I could keep my mouth shut or tell him and see how he reacted. "Kristin," I said as I took a free throw and made it.

"Nice choice. Have you told her yet?" He stole the ball right out of my hands and shot. He seemed to hang in the air as the ball followed a perfect arc to the net.

"Still trying to figure that out, Kyle. You know me, kind of 'dumb and dumber.'"

"Not dumb, hey-hey-HaberMAN, just out of practice," Kyle said, laughing.

"I was never *in* practice," I said. "I better head out of here. My mom will send trackers after me."

"Hang in there," Kyle yelled.

I jogged toward home, pleased that he hadn't seemed at all bothered when I mentioned Kristin. If Kristin liked him, he must not know it. I hurried, but I was still late. I knew what kind of happy greeting was waiting on me.

"Your dinner is getting cold, Aaron," Mom said, looking irritated.

"Aaron, how many times have we asked you to be on time for dinner?" Dad pressed his lips tightly together. He was trying not to yell while he was at the table.

"Lots, Dad." I quickly washed my hands in the sink and sat down. They were already half finished with dinner. Sarah had spaghetti sauce around her mouth. She stuck her tongue out at me, loving the fact that I was in trouble. I desperately wanted to fling just one meatball in her direction.

Kyle didn't have this problem. He could come in whenever he felt like it. I was too old to have this many rules. I ate my wilting salad and almost cold spaghetti. I didn't really want it, but I sure wanted to avoid any more trouble. At least for the rest of the night. I couldn't wait to escape to my room, turn on the radio, and totally zone out.

As I left the kitchen, Mom put her hand on my shoulder and asked, "Are you okay?"

"Sure, Mom," I lied.

"I'm around if you need to talk, you know," she said.

"Thanks. I'm just going to my room. Do a little reading for social studies." *And beat myself over the head with something,* I thought.

Maybe I should just forget about Kristin. There's always other prey in the jungle, my new tiger instinct told me. *Love 'em and leave 'em,* I thought. In my case it would be more like, Look at 'em and lose 'em. I pulled out the little hardbound yearbook from last year. Our school's PTA had a ton of money, so our school got to have a yearbook even though most elementary schools don't.

I flipped through last year's fifth graders twice. We had two new girls transfer in this year, but everyone else was right there in black and white. For the life of me, I didn't feel the slightest bit of interest in anyone but Kristin. Lots of girls were nice, many were cute, a few were funny. But the old heart didn't thump for anyone but this blonde, gray-eyed girl with the slightly crooked grin. I couldn't help it. It was fate or something.

I analyzed my own picture. Puffy brown hair that had a mind of its own. Brown eyes with too-long lashes, covered up by round wire-rim glasses. My grandmother had offered to buy me contacts. She and my mother kept telling me I was handsome and would be even more so if people could see my eyes. I didn't believe them and definitely did not want to stick anything on my eyeballs. I shuddered at the thought of it.

I fell asleep with the lights on and the yearbook on my chest. I dreamed of fast cars, basketball goals, and a tiger loose in our neighborhood.

Chapter 7

Scoot a Boot

On the way to art class the next morning, Jessica bumped into me in the hall and pressed a note into my hand. "Excuse me, Aaron," she said, never even looking at me.

I sat at the back of the room while the teacher was telling us what masterpiece we were going to paint that day. I quietly untangled the white notebook paper, which had been folded into a complicated triangle, every corner tucked back into itself somehow.

Dear Aaron,

Here is a ♪ from me. (Aren't you glad????) Well, I talked to you-know-who. Here's the scoop: she *loves* country music. Can you believe it? Well, believe it. Says she is crazy about cowboy boots too. Maybe you should ride a horse to school.

Ha, Ha, Ha. Later, gator! J.

Now, this was totally weird. Hardly anyone at our school listened to country music. Rap, alternative, rock, but not country so much. I had some work to do. And it wasn't going to be easy. I loved all music. Well, just about. Country was stretching it, though. It always sounded the same to me. Some guy loses his girl, his dog, his truck, and then he moans about it while he listens to sad music on a jukebox. Sometimes a girl singer is telling some guy to pack his bags and get lost.

After school, I asked Mom if we could stop by the mall.

"Well, it's not exactly on the way, Aaron. What do you need?"

"I need a CD," I said. "I'll spend my own money. Could you just, uh, lend it to me until we get home?"

"You *need* a CD? Or you *want* a CD?" She looked at her watch, and then at me.

"Believe me, I need it more than I want it." I sighed.

"Do you know which one? Can you run in really fast?"

"Well, actually, I could use a suggestion. What's a good country music CD?" I asked.

"Country? Since when do you like country?" She glanced at me and then changed lanes.

"I decided to expand my musical interests," I said.

"Any special reason?" she asked. She was raising one eyebrow.

"Kristin likes country. I thought I would give it a try." I might as well level with her on this one. Who knew? Maybe she had some advice I could use, for once.

"You sure you want to spend your own money? What if you don't like it?" she asked.

"I guess I could give it to Kristin if I don't." At least then I wouldn't be stuck with something I wouldn't listen to ever again. Yes, I was willing to spring for one CD. For the noble cause of love.

"Does Dad have any boots?" I wondered out loud.

"Western boots? Aaron, this is quite a transformation, I must say." Mom was smiling and I wasn't. But I needed assistance and had to humor her at the moment.

"I just wondered. Phil's dad wears them and says they are really comfortable." This was probably too much, asking her to believe I would follow fashion advice from Phil's father. He still wore green socks to match his green shirt, and long plaid shorts that showed his bony knees.

"Dad has an old pair from college, I think," Mom said.

He went to college in Texas, so I was hopeful. I wasn't so sure I could get up the nerve to wear them, though.

"Aaron. You know what I am going to say."

"Be myself." I made an effort not to roll my eyes. "Yes, Mom, I know. Maybe 'myself' has a sudden craving for twangy guitars and chewing tobacco." We both laughed.

We turned in to the mall and parked at the entrance near the music store. Mom got out too, but I ran ahead and went straight for the country artist section. I had never even dreamed of looking there before. The names were strange to me. This must be how adults feel when they wander into the rap section. Finally, I found one in the discount bin, *Greatest Country Hits.* A couple of names were familiar, maybe.

Mom paid for it, eyeing me suspiciously. "I'll just hold on to the receipt, Aaron. You can pay me as soon as we get home."

"No problem, Mom. Thanks a lot." I took the CD out of the bag and scanned the song titles, not knowing any of them. New experiences could be fun, I told myself. Yeah, an adventure where the buffalo roam. Yee haw.

I listened in the privacy of my own bedroom. Some of the songs made me laugh into my pillow as I rolled around on the bed and howled at my ceiling light fixture. A couple of the songs weren't so bad. In fact, I liked them a little by the second time I heard them. But I knew I wouldn't admit that to just anyone. I had my reputation to consider. I was sure risking it, all to impress Kristin.

Mom tapped on my door. When I opened it, she was holding up the receipt in one hand and holding out her other hand, palm up. "Well, what do you think of it?" she asked.

I dug through my old spaceship money bank until I found enough crumpled bills and quarters to pay her back. "I guess it's okay, Mom, but I can only take it for a little while. Then I go crazy. The songs sound pretty much alike."

"Yeah, I know what you mean." She pointed to my CD collection, grinned, and left.

I went into their bedroom closet and found the boots, dusty and forgotten, way in back. I pulled them on and tried to walk around. They were a little too big and very heavy.

I clumped awkwardly down the hall. My jeans were not made

for boots, so I stuffed them down inside. Faded suede patches in diamond shapes decorated the boot tops.

I looked in the full-length mirror on the back of the bathroom door. *Oh, yeah,* I thought. *I really look hot in these.* I looked like an idiot. *I'm in a two-toned western shirt and alligator-skin boots, like the country stars wear on their CD covers. As I stand against a fence on my million-dollar ranch, I hook my thumbs in the matching alligator belt. The roar of my private helicopter announces the arrival of a very special dinner guest: Miss Kristin Kramer.*

Sarah peeked in on me. "You look stupid," she said.

I figured she was right.

Chapter 8

A Fool for Love

As soon as my alarm went off, I jumped out of bed and pulled out every pair of old jeans I could find, looking for a pair I could wear with the boots. The legs had to be big enough to pull down over the boot tops. One old pair of jeans was too tight in the waist and I couldn't zip them up all the way, but the pant legs worked, so I threw on a baggy old T-shirt that was pretty long.

Was I actually going to do this? I was beginning to wonder if my brain was scratched up or something. Like a bad CD. I went in to breakfast, forgetting that I might get a reaction in my own house.

Sarah started laughing and spewed juice onto her shirt. Mom wasn't overly thrilled about that and gave me a quick up-and-down look as she wiped Sarah clean.

"Are you pretending to be a cowboy?" Sarah asked. "Yee haw!" she yelled. "Where's your horsey?"

"Quiet, dog breath," I growled, not noticing that Dad was still at home.

"Aaron. Watch your mouth!" Dad growled louder. "Are those my boots?"

"Well, please make her leave me alone. Yes, can I borrow them?" I asked.

"I guess so, Aaron. But it is customary to ask permission *before* you borrow something," he said, looking back down at the newspaper.

Like he ever wore them. Like I was borrowing something that was important to him. But I just said, "Thanks, Dad" and clumped over to grab a bowl and the box of cereal.

"What's the occasion?" Dad asked as he glanced at my mother over the rim of his coffee cup.

"I just felt like … wearing boots today." I began eating cereal, hoping to avoid any further questions about my wardrobe.

"Aren't they a little big?" Mom asked.

"They're okay," I slurped. I saw her look at Dad and shrug. I was pretty sure this was a clue to him that maybe they should drop the subject. I hoped so.

On the way to school, Mom tried real hard not to bring up the fact that I looked like a cowboy version of a nerd. She had this worried look around the eyebrows, and I saw her bite her bottom lip a couple of times. Finally she said, "Hope you have a … good day, Aaron," as I got out of the car.

"Yeah, I hope I do too, Mom." And off I stomped, up the steps to school. I sure hoped Jessica was right. This was potentially the dumbest thing I had ever done, otherwise.

The abuse started as soon as I walked into the main hall.

"I believe I smell a cow patty," said someone behind me. I didn't even turn around.

"Aaron!" Wild laughter. "What in the world are you doing in those?" Alicia Brown asked as she ran up to me.

I tried to give her a dirty look, but she was laughing so hard, I'm not sure she saw it.

"Hey, uh, nice boots," Phil said. I glanced at him to see if he was serious, because you never know with Phil.

"Thanks, Phil." I was trying to get to my seat as quickly as possible so I could sit down.

Larry Shumberg stopped when he got to my desk, looked down at the boots, and then looked back up at me. "Man," he said. "And I thought *I* dressed bad." Chuckling to himself, he wandered over to his own seat.

I was watching the door, wondering where Kristin was. It was almost time for the tardy bell. I was sitting with my feet stuck out straight in front of my desk so she would see the boots if she came in. Everyone who passed by laughed at me. Jessica walked past and sat down. She pulled out a pink slip of paper and wrote something. She folded it three or four times and passed it to me.

Glancing at the teacher to make sure she wasn't watching, I opened the note.

> Dear A. Boots are a nice touch. They look a little old, though.
>
> Good luck! J.

The bell rang and Ms. Newhouse called roll. No Kristin. Maybe she was only late. Oh, *please* don't let her be absent today, of all days. Oh, man, was I making a fool of myself for nothing? So far, it certainly looked that way.

Up until about eleven o'clock, I still hoped she might show up. I almost asked if I could go to the office and call my mom to bring me a pair of Nikes. I had a feeling she would tell me to hang in there, that I could make it until the day was over. I wasn't up for a "be yourself, even if you are wearing boots" lecture. So I suffered through the day. And I do mean suffered.

I have come to the conclusion that PE is impossible in cowboy boots. I don't know how the cowboys managed to chase down their horses or run to the chuck wagon for dinner or do anything else they had to do. I felt like I had a lump of concrete on each foot. I had on three pairs of socks because the boots were too big, so my feet were boiling hot. And the zipper in my jeans kept sliding down because the waist was too tight to button. Everyone kept looking at me weird. I was either stomping around loudly or trying to pull up my zipper without anyone seeing. This went on all day.

I hoped Kyle wouldn't see me in the boots, but he caught me right at the end of lunch. "Aaron, I don't know how to break this to you, but ... Lose the shoes, dude ... A babe magnet they are *not!*" he whispered as he walked behind me to throw his trash away.

"It's a long story, Kyle," I said.

"Well, I would stick around and hear the story, Hey-Hey-Haber-MAN, but I gotta rustle me some cattle." Kyle laughed at himself and pretended to gallop off. A crowd of sixth-grade boys cheered him on, waving imaginary lassos and hats in the air and yelling, "Yippee-KI-ay! Yee, doggies," and other weird cowboy-type things. Who knows what those things meant? I didn't care. I just wanted to follow my dirty napkin and crumpled lunch sack right into the trash can.

Chapter 9

Golden Moldies

I almost made it home, to safety. As I was getting out of my car, very ready to run into the house and hide the dreaded boots in the attic, here came Chris. He had come over to tell me about the celebrity cousin in LA. He took one look at my boots and started laughing. He couldn't stop. I think he tried, but he was bent over, and every time he rose up and saw me, he started all over again. He was laughing so hard, he was crying.

Shaking his head and wiping his eyes, he said, "Sorry, Aaron ... I just ..." and he doubled over again. His shoulders were shaking. He put his hand over his mouth, trying to squash in the snorting laughter. He shook his head from side to side, knowing he wasn't going to be able to stop anytime soon.

When I closed my front door, I could still hear him. There was no point in being mad at him. I knew I looked ridiculous in the huge old boots. I just wasn't the cowboy-boot type, and he certainly wasn't either. There had to be some other way to make an impression on Kristin. Something less damaging to whatever reputation I had left.

Since it was Friday afternoon, I was off the hook for putting in homework time. I decided to take a long jog over to Kristin's house. Maybe take a portable CD player with me and listen to some tunes on the way. I would have to dig it out of the storage closet, but I was pretty sure we still had one. Mom had been quiet, sensing that my day was the kind that I would like to permanently block from my memory.

I changed jeans and put the rotten old boots back in Dad's closet, under a sack of Halloween costumes. I wouldn't need them again. I grabbed the new CD from my room, found a player and batteries, and put on some beloved old Nikes. Running through the kitchen, I yelled, "See you later, Mom. I'm going to take a walk."

It was a long way to her house but I didn't care. When I finally got there, it looked pretty quiet. So I circled back around, twice. The third time I went by, Kristin was sitting on her front steps, looking through the day's mail.

"Hi, Kristin. How are ya feeling?" I called out.

"I'm okay now. Just had a sore throat this morning and my mom made me stay home," she said. "Did I miss anything?"

"It was … a pretty dull day," I said. What a lie.

"That's not exactly what I heard." She was smiling at me crookedly. "Who are you listening to?"

"Oh, just some country golden moldies." I adjusted my headphones.

"Golden moldies?"

"Yeah, you know, country oldies ... CD," I said.

"Country?" She looked puzzled.

"Yeah," I said, figuring she was all surprised that I liked "her" kind of music.

"I didn't know you liked country stuff. I, uh, heard about the boots today. I was kind of surprised. I thought you were more a rap or rock kind of guy," she said quietly.

"Oh, yeah, I'm really into country. Rap and rock are okay too. But give me an old boot-kickin' song any day." I nodded along with the beat.

"That's ... interesting, Aaron," Kristin said. "Well, I better go back in. My mom said I have to take it easy for the rest of the day. See ya." She waved as she walked toward her door. She looked back at me with that same, squinty-eyed, puzzled look. She smiled for just a second and disappeared inside her house.

This was not exactly the response I had expected. I thought she would say, "Oh, wow! I love country music too! Finally someone understands! Finally, I have a soul mate! Come in and let's listen together!" Some things like that. Maybe she was shy, like I was. Or maybe her throat was still hurting. At least we had talked, in a way.

When I got back home, I called Jessica.

"I can't believe she was absent, Jessica. I did the boot thing for nothing," I said.

"Oh, she knows you wore them, Aaron. Everyone's talking about it," Jessica said, laughing.

"Don't remind me, Jessica. Please. I need some other inside information. I just can't handle the boots again."

"Hmm ..." Jessica paused. "She does also love ice skating."

"Oh, no. I can't ice-skate. I hate it. I would fall flat on my butt."

"Well, she loves it, that's all I can say," Jessica said a little snottily.

"Okay, okay. Thanks. I'll talk to you later, Jess."

"Are you going to ask her to go skating? Are you going to the rink at the mall?" she asked quickly.

I groaned. "I guess so. Maybe tomorrow afternoon. Oh, this is gonna be bad."

"It will be fun! Do it, Aaron!"

"I'll talk to you later," I said again, hanging up this time.

Perfect. Why did Kristin have to like everything I hated? They say opposites attract, but I never understood what these opposites were supposed to talk about if that was true. I didn't know anything about country music, and I could barely walk in the boots, and I couldn't ice-skate. I would look like a two-year-old out there. Totally uncoordinated. Why couldn't she like basketball?

I stopped by to talk to Chris, hoping he was over his laughing fit by now. He was, and I told him my problem. Chris was always good about suggesting solutions to impossible situations.

"Well, since you can't ice-skate, and she loves to, you have to make sure you don't have to skate but that you still get credit for asking her," he said.

"Huh?" I didn't quite follow him.

"I mean, ask her, and then ... have a little accident so you don't have to skate," said Chris, proud of himself that he had offered such a simple plan.

"What do you mean by 'a little accident'? Like fall and break my leg?" I was getting worried.

"No, man, just kind of twist your ankle or something. She'll be all sorry for you and maybe be willing to just forget it and go have some ice cream together." Chris was beaming. He loved counseling people like this.

This sounded pretty workable to me. And I didn't even have to wear boots. But I did have to make a phone call. I had to call Kristin's house and invite her. Was I a man or a mouse? A tough kid or a puny chicken? A winner or a wimp? All of the above, I decided.

Chapter 10

Dare to Dial

My armpits were damp and sticky. My throat seemed to be lined with felt. Somehow I managed to punch in Kristin's phone number. Before it rang, I hung up. At least I hoped it hadn't rung yet. I did some deep breathing and almost got dizzy, little black circles starting to close in on my line of sight.

I lay on the floor and waited to feel normal. Figuring that would never really happen, I got up and tried again. Hoping Kristin would answer the phone and hoping she wouldn't, both at the same time.

"Hello?" It was her *dad*.

Kiss me good-bye. *He may shoot me. Threaten to strangle my scrawny neck. Have a cop come to my door and arrest me for ... calling his daughter.*

"Hello?" he answered again.

"May I ... uh ... Could I please ... you know ... talk to Kristin?" I closed my eyes as tightly as I could, sure that he would say, "No way! Stupid kid! Leave her alone!"

"Sure, just a second," he said. "Kris-tin, tell-e-phone," he yelled.

I put my hand over my eyes. Sure, I was still alive, but I hadn't asked her yet. Anything could happen at this point. There were no guarantees. I should have come up with a plan B. She was probably going to say, "No way! Stupid jerk! Leave me alone!"

"Hello?" the soft voice floated through the fog in my head.

Be casual, Aaron. Be normal. Okay, scratch that. Just talk to her. Good grief. How hard can it be? *Oh, about as hard as rock climbing without using your feet*, I thought.

"Hey, uh, Kristin. What's up?" That was dumb—I had just talked to her about an hour before.

"Aaron?"

So much for my phone manners. "Yeah, it's me," I said.

"Hi," she said, and giggled. It sounded a little like music.

"I was going to be at the mall tomorrow, and if you were there, we might run into each other and stuff." *Real smooth*, I thought.

"Oh, I *love* to go to the mall," she said. "I'll have to ask my parents, and convince them I'm well. But it's not like I had fever or anything. Hold on ..." She was gone a long time. I could hear them talking in the background, but couldn't really understand what they were saying. I heard my name once and "Oh, Mom, *please!*"

She came back on the line and said in an excited voice, "Yes! I can. Only, I have to go in a group. Can we ask some other people to come too?"

"Sure," I said. Hey, invite the whole Marine Corps for all I cared. She was going to go!

"You call whoever you want," I said. "What time do you want to meet at the rink?"

"The rink?" she asked, sounding like I had just said, "Meet at the North Pole."

"Yeah, we can get some ice skating in and then have some ice cream and hit the music store. Check out the country section," I answered.

The line was mysteriously quiet. "Kristin?" I asked.

"Uh yeah, I guess that's okay, Aaron." She sounded like she had just flushed a pet turtle down the toilet.

I couldn't imagine what on earth was wrong. "Are you sure?" I asked.

"Oh, yeah, that's okay. I'll call a couple of people and you call some and we can meet about two o'clock," she said, sounding a little better.

"Great! At the rink, tomorrow at two!" I was smiling so big, the corners of my mouth began to hurt.

"Sure … at the … rink," Kristin sighed. "See you tomorrow."

I hung up and quickly forgot how unhappy she had sounded, being drenched by my own tidal wave of pure joy. I jumped up and down. Leaped and skipped around the house. Even grabbed up Sarah and swung her around. She laughed and followed me around for five minutes nagging me to "Do it again!" I finally had to tell her (nicely) to shut up and leave me alone. I needed time to lie on my bed, think about everything, and soak up my good luck like warm sunlight after a cold rain.

The minor fact that I could ice-skate about as well as three-legged beagle had momentarily slipped my mind.

Chapter 11

Have a Nice Trip

I got to the ice rink about twenty minutes before Kristin was supposed to meet me. I wanted time to get my skates on and figure out how I was going to pull this off. I had forgotten how cold it always was in the rink area and had worn only a short-sleeved T-shirt with my jeans. I had to keep rubbing my arms to get warm. The attendant helped me lace up my skates, and I tried to stand up. It was pretty easy. I could walk around on the rubber mat with only a little wobbling.

Maybe I could do it after all. I would just admit to Kristin that I hadn't skated in a long time (like never) and was out of practice. I inched my way over to the edge of the ice. Gripping the bar at the top of the low wall, I eased out, one tiny step at a time. My foot slipped and I almost went down, but I recovered and stood, facing the wall, with both hands locked on the bar.

I tried to turn around, and just as I was letting go with one hand, some hotshot raced past me, so close I could feel the wind. Losing what little balance I had, I waved my arms around wildly and my legs flew up. I landed right on my cheeks, and I don't mean my face. I felt a deep red flush from my neck up and crawled back over to the safety of the rubber floor.

It was hard enough to walk on ice with a full rubber-soled foot. How was I supposed to manage on only a thin little blade? This was not only impossible but ridiculous. *So, now what?* I wondered.

I made it over to a bench and sat down, desperately trying to think. I could not possibly let Kristin see me on the ice. I would fall in two seconds. She would never respect me after that. Phil was supposed to show up too, but I knew better than to count on that. If he did come, maybe he could help somehow.

"There's Aaron!" Jessica's voice carried over the noisy concession area. She was dressed in a hot-pink skating outfit and walked confidently over, wearing her own snow-white ice skates. Kristin followed along behind her, dressed in red sweats and sneakers. "Hey, Aaron, ready to hit the ice?" Jessica winked at me.

I already did, I thought. "Just … taking a break, Jess. I've been here awhile. Hi, Kristin. Are you feeling okay today?" I asked, pretending to be slightly out of breath from my rigorous skating.

"I feel fine, Aaron. Are you okay?" Kristin asked.

"Yeah, sure, why?" I began to feel a small twinge in my gut.

"We saw you take that nasty tumble, Aaron," Jessica said. "I bet you hit a patch of loose ice."

My stomach twisted again, and a hot blast of misery shot up into my head. I couldn't even look at Kristin. She had seen me fall. She had seen me crawl. She knew the awful truth.

I stood up, saying, "Oh, that. I just slipped on something. No big ... AHHHH!" I was leaning against the bench and, unsteady on the skates, started to fall backward. The last thing I saw before hitting my head on the floor behind the bench was this horrified look on Kristin's face.

Maybe I passed out for a couple of seconds, or maybe I just wanted to. When I opened my eyes again, the manager of the ice rink was leaning over me, and I heard Phil's voice saying, "I know him, he's my neighbor."

"Well, can you give me his parents' number so I can call them?" the manager was asking Phil.

I tried to tell them I was okay, but they weren't listening to me. I didn't see Kristin or Jessica. They hadn't even stuck around to see if I was alive. Phil helped me up and I sat on the bench, my head hanging down into my hands. The manager must have gone to call my mom or dad.

"Oh gosh, Aaron, are you okay?" Phil asked, concern making his voice a little shaky.

"Physically I'm okay, Phil. Did you see Kristin and Jessica?"

"They went to get something to drink. The manager was telling everyone to back away from you. Oh, here they come."

I looked but didn't see any place I could hide. Kristin and Jessica were walking in our direction, both of them with worried expressions. Jessica was carrying a drink and a straw.

"Tell them I had to go to the bathroom," I said, hobbling toward the restroom as fast as I could on my skates. Once I got safely inside, I sat down on the floor and took off my skates. I sat, leaning up against the bathroom wall, trying to figure out a way to be teleported directly to my house.

I close my eyes, and when I open them, I am in a hospital bed, the room a stark white. Friends are gathered around my bed, waiting eagerly for my eyes to open at last. Vaguely familiar voices are whispering.

"What will we do without Aaron?"

"We didn't appreciate him. I feel so awful."

"He's the best friend I've ever had."

"I never even told him I loved him."

The last comment is from Kristin, who is dabbing her eyes with a tissue.

I struggle to open my swollen eyes, unable to move because my entire body is covered with bandages. Kristin leans over and grasps my hand, tears filling her eyes. Phil and Chris and Kyle and Jessica are there.

Alicia Brown and Larry Shumberg look at each other and say, "He's faking." Lousy daydream—what are *they* doing in it?

I must have been in the bathroom a long time, because finally Phil came in and said, "Your dad is here. What happened to you anyway?"

"I managed to make a bigger fool out of myself than I did on the famous 'boot day.'"

"How did you fall?" Phil wondered aloud.

"I tripped," I said.

"Over what?" he asked.

"Over my own stupidity," I said, knowing I could never, ever show my face in public again.

Chapter 12

Cover Me

"Aaron? Are you in there?" Dad's voice came from the other side of the bathroom door.

"Just a minute," I groaned. Phil pulled on my arm, trying to get me to stand up.

"Go out and scout around and see if Jessica and Kristin are gone, Phil. Hurry."

As Phil opened the door, Dad walked in. "Are you okay?" he asked.

"Get me out of here, Dad. Is there a back door?" What would I do if there wasn't?

"No, Aaron, let's just go. Mom will not be happy if I don't take you to the doctor. Did you fall on your head?" He had a real pained look on his face, maybe like this was a problem he didn't need and maybe like he was worried about me.

Phil came to the door and whispered, "They're still here, Aaron."

I saw that Dad was carrying a sweater. "I need your sweater, quick."

He must have been a little rattled, because he just handed it to me without even asking why.

I stuck the blue sweater over my head and handed my skates to Phil. "Turn these in for me and grab my Nikes." It was now or never.

"Uh, what are you doing, Aaron?" Dad was probably worried that my brains had been scrambled in the fall.

I eased out the bathroom door and almost immediately heard Jessica's and Kristin's voices.

"Are you all right?" Kristin asked. I felt a hand on my arm. Was it hers? I couldn't see because of the sweater covering my head.

"Aaron! What happened? Are you okay? Why do you have a sweater on your head?" Jessica was talking fast.

"I'm okay. After a fall, you should … just … cover your eyes. They can be very sensitive to the light."

I heard Dad groan a little, but at least he didn't blow my cover, or take the sweater, either.

"I'll call you later and see how you are." Unfortunately this was Jessica's voice again.

Somehow we made it to the car, and I immediately slid down to the floorboard in the backseat. Phil got back there with me.

"Are they looking?" I whispered to Phil.

"Who? Oh … No, they're still inside the mall," he answered.

"Thanks, Dad. And by the way, I'm really fine." I removed the sweater and spit some blue fuzz out that had stuck to my lips.

"I think we better have you checked, Aaron," Dad insisted. "Can you imagine what Mom will say when she gets back if we *don't* go to a clinic?"

Good point. I would rather suffer a doctor visit than have both my head and Dad's examined by a mad mom.

We ended up stopping by a little clinic and calling Phil's mother to let her know he was with us. The doctor there looked in my eyeballs for a long time. Apparently he didn't see any huge brain lump or anything, because he said I could go home. They just had to wake me up several times during the night. I guess this was to make sure I didn't go into a coma or drool or whatever.

Mom kept wanting to know what had happened, but how could I explain it? I wasn't even sure myself. One minute I thought I had things under control, and the next I was lying on the ground behind a bench, with the girl I loved staring at me with horrified, bugged-out eyes.

I spent a miserable night, between being shaken awake about ten times by my parents and then dreaming about ice skating in a pink tutu with popcorn-eating crowds staring and laughing at me. By the time Mom came in to wake me for school, I felt pretty sure I looked bad enough to get out of going.

"My head hurts a little, but mainly I'm just exhausted, you know? Maybe I better rest today."

"Okay, baby, go back to sleep." She stroked my hair and quietly slipped out.

A semi-coma sounded almost useful right about now. At least

then I couldn't think about my pathetic life. I wouldn't have to face seeing the kids at school. Maybe by the time I came out of the coma, they would forget. *I imagine everyone's excitement as my eyes finally flutter open after many years. Phil and Chris are here, with beards and suits. My dad says, "At last, he's awake. I knew buying that Hummer for him would come in handy."*

Mom says, "Darling, Time *magazine wants to do a story on you and wonders if you would like to form your own band." And of course, Kristin is there, holding roses and crying, "I am so glad I waited for him."*

I pulled the sheet over my head and went back to sleep, hoping I wouldn't dream again about jeering crowds or tigers on ice skates, skating better than I did.

* * * * * * * * * *

Later that afternoon, I heard a timid knock at my door. Figuring it was Phil, I just ignored it and tried to doze off again. Kristin's voice floated around my head: "Aaron, are you awake?"

Ahh, this might be a nice dream, I thought, trying to slip deeper into sleep.

"Aaron, I just wanted to stop by and see if you were okay," Kristin's dreamy voice continued.

About that time a large object flew through the air and landed on the end of my bed. I sat straight up and saw two females in my room. My dippy sister Sarah was grinning as she sat, crushing my feet, and Kristin stood beside the bed staring at my hair, which was no doubt sticking straight up into the air. It does that every time I sleep.

I was really trying to figure out if I was dreaming again. Then Kristin laughed and asked, "How are you? Did I wake you up? Or is that a stupid question?" and I realized this wasn't sounding very much like a dream anymore. I slid back down onto my pillow, hoping my hair would be hidden a little. I also tried to quietly kick my sister off the bed while I managed to smile at Kristin.

I knew I was blushing again because my face got really hot, but I hoped she would think it was because of my head injury. "No, I was awake. How was school?"

"Boring, as usual. Everyone was talking about you, Aaron, and wondering how you were. I just wanted to stop by and make sure you were okay." She smiled sweetly, as only Kristin could. "I brought you a couple of my books, for when you're lying around. I read a lot of science fiction and figured you might like them. I remembered you dressed as an android for Halloween and ..."

"I love science fiction! Cool!" I said, taking the books from her.

"Will you be back at school tomorrow?" she asked.

"I might not ever come back." I closed my eyes and sighed real big.

"Why?" She got that worried-eyebrow look like my mom gets.

"Well, I feel a little stupid," I said.

"Gosh, Aaron, you shouldn't. But I know what you mean. I tripped one time when we were going into this restaurant. There was this whole basketball team coming out, and I fell right in front of them. I think I turned blood red and for a long time hated going back there. My parents kept saying it was no big deal, but *they* weren't the ones who had kissed the concrete in front of an audience." She was laughing.

I laughed too and said, "Yeah, I guess I'll probably go back to school someday. Maybe after the next math test."

It was so nice to be laughing with her that I forgot I probably looked like I had a hairy chipmunk on my head.

"Maybe we can try the rink again sometime, and I'll try to stay on my feet," I said.

"Yeah, Aaron. Uh … but … I'm not really big on ice skating. I'm sorry, but I haven't ever really learned how, and …"

"What?" I sat back up again, my hair suddenly not important. "I thought you loved ice skating!"

"Who told you that?" Kristin asked.

"Jessica," I said, the wheels beginning to slowly turn in my head.

"Now, why would she do that, I wonder?" Kristin looked confused.

"That's what I'd like to know. And I think I'll find out."

Chapter 13

Just Say It

I couldn't wait to have a little chat with Jessica. Being angry made me forget about being embarrassed at school. Everyone came up to me either laughing or asking if my head was broken.

"Skating can be dangerous. And so can friends," I said, watching the classroom door for Jessica to show up.

She bounced in and started to rush over to me, smiling like she'd just had a bowl of whipped cream. When she saw the look on my face, she stopped and her smile crumpled. The teacher told us to sit down just as the tardy bell rang, so she didn't have a chance to ask me what was going on.

We had an assembly that morning. Some high school group was coming to dance and sing for us. I was really not in the mood for that. I made sure I was behind Jessica as we lined up to go to the cafeteria. She seemed a little nervous, and I was glad.

I pretended to be extremely interested in the show until the music got really loud. We were sitting at the back of the cafeteria, since we were sixth graders and supposedly tall enough to see over all the little kids.

"Hey, Jes. I have a little question for you," I whispered near her head.

"Sure, Aaron. Are you better? You look mad. What's wrong?" She looked like I might pull out some small device and use it to torture her.

"Boy, you were so right about Kristin and ice skating. She just loves it. Told me about all the trophies she had won. Yeah, you called that one right, Jessica." I stared at her with a face that I hoped looked particularly evil.

She looked down at her lap. Obviously she couldn't think of anything to say.

"What's the matter, Jessica? Have anything you'd like to tell me? Hmm?" I said right next to her ear.

I know she was wondering if I knew she had lied. Wondering if she was trapped or if she could fake it. I guess she decided I looked mad enough that she better not lie again.

"I'm sorry, Aaron." Her voice was barely a whisper.

"I'm sorry, Jessica, I couldn't quite hear you."

"I said I'm sorry, Aaron." Her voice was getting a little irritated. The truth hurts sometimes.

"Any particular reason why you lied like a dog, my *good* friend?" I sneered.

"Yes, but, I … I just wanted …" She was good and miserable. I began to feel a little better.

"Yeah, let's hear it. What *did* you want?" I asked, glancing over to see if any teacher was watching our little conversation.

The music was loud and everyone was clapping in rhythm. I was having a different kind of fun. Nailing a liar.

Suddenly Jessica seemed to get mad too. "Because I liked you and I thought if you would just get over Miss Blonde Perfection, well …," she said very quickly, looking out at the dancers on stage, twirling and leaping.

I was totally stunned. Jessica liking me? We had just been friends, and I had never really even talked that much to her. But then Kristin had never talked that much to me either, and that didn't stop me from being crazy about her. I had no idea what to say.

"Oh" was my intelligent response.

Suddenly I wondered if Jessica had lied about other things too.

"But Kristin does like country music? And boots?" I asked.

"Well, maybe she does. I mean, she likes a lot of things."

I stared at Jessica, hoping my eyes were laser beams into her brain.

"Okay, okay! She doesn't like it at all. Sorry!" Jessica was disgusted with me, herself, and probably life in general. I knew how that felt.

"Why did you have to be this big game player, Jessica? Why didn't you just say what you wanted to say instead of making up all this junk?"

She glared right back at me. "Well, I could ask you the same thing, couldn't I, Aaron?"

Yep, she had a point. I had been the all-time game player. Boots and all. Tiger in a chicken suit, that's me. I had a vision of my mom's face saying, "Just be yourself, Aaron" for the gazillionith time. I squinted my eyes shut to block it out. Nobody likes good advice.

Everyone was up and giving the group a standing ovation. We filed out and back to class. I had a lot to think about that day. Like the idea of saying what I felt. Talking instead of stalking. That would take a whole lot of courage. I was better at imagining and pretending, but hey, I could give it a try.

There was a long line into the cafeteria at lunch, and sure enough, out of habit, I zoned out again. *I ride up to a grand castle on my muscular black horse. I dismount and rap on the huge wooden door. Removing my gloves, I tell the servant, "I have come to call on Lady Kramer." He shows me in and Kristin is coming down the stone staircase. She is dressed in one of those flowing dresses, with a tall hat that looks like a giant upside-down ice-cream cone. Gorgeous, of course. "I have come to tell you my intentions, my lady," I say as I take a deep bow.*

"Yes, and what might they be, Lord Haberman?" She blinks her eyes really fast.

"I would like us to be ... uh ... to go ... out," I say. I must have said this out loud, as Alicia Brown was standing next to me in the lunch line and said, "What?"

"Nothing, Alicia. I mean, way *to go*, they are probably *out* of cake by now."

Close one. I should remember to daydream alone. I never knew I talked.

Chapter 14

Out on a Limb

I went over to Phil's after school to shoot some baskets. He wasn't a master player like Kyle, but he had more room to shoot in his driveway than I did.

"So, how's it going, Aaron?" Phil dribbled and attempted a goofy shot behind his back, which he did not make.

"Okay, I guess. I am just getting tired of always messing up."

"Messing up what?" Phil was tall and lanky and could dunk almost without jumping. He tried this and somehow managed to miss. But Phil never got upset.

"Messing up about Kristin." I leaped into the air and tried to dunk, missing it also.

"Oh, you still like her?" Phil was very, very quick about picking up on what was going on around him.

"*Yes*, Phil. That's, like, the reason I have been making a fool of myself. Hoping I could get her attention and that she would figure out I like her."

"Well, why don't you just tell her?" Phil was inexperienced with girls. He didn't realize his idea was very bizarre.

Still, perhaps he had a point. What if, as a totally new plan, I just *told her*? *I just walk up and say, "Hey, you, Kristin. I think you're special. Let's go out." And she says, "Oh, Aaron, I have been hoping you would say that. I think about you every day and every night. You are the best … at everything!"*

Of course, I couldn't just walk up and say that. I would probably quiver and choke and melt like the Wicked Witch of the West in *The Wizard of Oz*. Not too impressive.

"I couldn't just walk up and say that, Phil. These things don't work like that." I clued old Phil in to the ways of the world.

"Then write her a note, dummy." Phil gave himself a high five with both hands after he made a distant shot. I don't think I have ever seen anyone but Phil do that. The self–high five, I mean.

A note. Hmm, had to hand it to Phil. The simplicity of it. I could say it, yet not have to say it. I could write pretty well. Yes, I would move on to Operation Tiger, Phase Two: Communication.

I went home and had dinner and then headed for my desk. I had to move all the junk off so I could find a flat place to write. By junk, I mean all my school stuff. I ripped a piece of notebook paper out of a spiral. It looked pretty ragged. This was, after all, for the love of my life, so I even went to the trouble to grab some scissors and cut off the torn edge. This was going to be the perfect note.

Thirty minutes later, I was still sitting there, playing with the pencil, doodling baskets and tigers in the margins. How could this be so hard to write? "Dear Kristin, I like you. Let's go out.

Bye, Aaron." No glow, no poetry. Just communication, raw and simple. And dull. I went into the den and looked for a book of quotations. My teacher last year had written quotes on the board every day.

I looked up *love, courage, hope,* and *basketball.* I was not inspired. Maybe a cookie would kick my brain into "think" mode. I went into the kitchen and hit the jackpot. Dad had brought home a bag of Looky Looky, Such Great Cookies from the mall. There is nothing better in this world than a cinnamon oatmeal chocolate chip LLSGC cookie.

As the dream cookie melted in my mouth, I closed my eyes and imagined sharing this perfect cookie with Kristin.

That was it! A "cookie date" at the mall. That's what I could put in the letter. An invitation for the perfect cookie to the perfect girl. *I gallantly walk up to the LLSGC counter and order two jumbo cinnamon oatmeal chocolate chip cookies and one super-cola with two straws. The tall cookie guy says, "It's on the house, Aaron. You are one of our best customers, not to mention one of the coolest guys I know." I hand Kristin her cookie. Our hands just barely touch. We sit down at a quiet table in the corner and smile into each other's eyes. When we lean over to drink from both our straws at the same time, we lightly bump heads. We laugh and her eyes crinkle at the corners. Some old song is playing in the background, the kind that girls love. Kristin thinks, This song reminds me of Aaron. It is without a doubt the best of days.*

I raced back to the desk and wrote:

Dear Kristin,

I hope this won't come as a big surprise, but I have liked you for a long time. Will you meet me at the mall, at the LLSGC counter at 2:00 PM on Saturday? If you are totally bummed out by this invitation, just tie an ugly-colored ribbon on the tree at the side of your house. And I will know you are, well, totally bummed out.

If you can come and think this is a cool idea, just meet me there.

Your not-so-secret admirer,

Aaron

Now, for the final execution of this plan, I had to consider ideal, dramatic placement of the note. Hide it on her desk at school? No, someone else might see it. Stuff it in her backpack? No, it might get lost. Hand it to her? No way. I would be brave when I had to be—like at the cookie counter, but certainly not yet. I would ... put it ... on the tree right in front of her house. She would see it when she went into her front door. It would work nicely with the tree theme and her tying a ribbon in the side-yard tree. Of course, ideally, she wouldn't be doing that.

I put the letter in a blue envelope I found on my parents' desk. And told my mom I would be right back, that I had to tell Phil something.

"It's getting a little late, isn't it, Aaron?" my dad asked as I bolted out the front door.

"I'll be back in just a minute." I smiled at him and closed the door before he could say anything else.

As I ran past Phil's house, I yelled, "Hey, Phil, I am going to Kristin's. See ya" to the house in general. Well, I *had* told my parents I needed to tell Phil something. It was a long way to Kristin's, but worth the trip.

Once I got there, I snuck up to the tree and took a long time to choose just the right side to stick the note on. It wasn't supposed to rain, so I would leave it that night and she should get it the next day. I had forgotten to bring a nail or whatever, so I just stuck a little limb through the envelope. I shook the limb until I felt sure the note wouldn't fall off. Then I ran back to my house, feeling proud and scared and worried and great.

Well, it was up to her now. I had stuck my feelings there, going out on a limb in more ways than one.

Chapter 15

Project Cookie

I told my mom I wanted to go to school early and would rather walk. I jogged over to Kristin's house, which wasn't easy with a heavy backpack. The note was gone. *Good*, I thought. Or maybe it was bad. That meant she had seen it, or maybe her parents had. In the meantime, I was going to be late for school.

I now had to run back in the other direction, toward school, with the backpack pounding my back with every step. I began to wonder if this had been such a good idea. When I got back to our street, Phil's mom was just leaving to take Phil to school. They were obviously running real late. She motioned for me to hop in. If she wondered why I was coming from the wrong end of the block, she didn't ask. Maybe she thought I had been out jogging with a backpack to build up my strength. Yeah, right.

Nervously, I entered my classroom, wondering what Kristin was going to say. She didn't even look up when I came in. She was copying the morning assignments from the board. I tried to act casual. I tried that all day. She was friendly, smiling and waving when we were in opposite ends of the line going to PE, but that was it. Tomorrow was Saturday and I had no idea if Kristin would be joining me for a cookie and the beginning of a relationship.

If my note had rocked her world, I couldn't tell it. What if she hadn't seen it? What if someone else had found it? *Her parents find the note, open it, and decide that I, Aaron, am a crazed maniac who is stalking their daughter! A crazed maniac cleverly disguised as a normal sixth grader. You can't be too careful these days, they think. We better move to Arizona, just to be safe. Kristin, sorry, but this is for your own protection, they say. She blinks back tears, but she has no choice but to go with them.*

As soon as school was out, I dumped my backpack at home and wandered over to Kristin's. My heart was thumping as I approached her house. Would there be some crud-colored ribbon tied to the tree beside her house? Would it all be over before it even started?

I walked by and didn't see a ribbon, but just in case I missed it, I ran back and into the side yard. I circled the tree, running, and just kept going. No ribbon. Awesome! Looky Looky, Such Great Cookies, here we come.

*　　*　　*　　*　　*　　*　　*　　*　　*　　*

On Saturday morning, I had the pleasure of doing chores, including folding laundry, cleaning my room, and helping my dad clean out the garage. I kept leaving the garage to check the clock. I was *not* going to be late to the mall. Mom had agreed to drop me off. She was a wonderful accomplice and didn't even know it.

"You taking medicine, Aaron?" was Dad's comment every time I ran into the kitchen to look at the clock. This was his attempt to be humorous, but he really needed some new material.

"No, Dad, I just don't want to be late."

"Very conscientious of you, son. But first let's get this project finished, or you're not going anywhere." Dad was very project oriented. Everything was a project, and most of the time I was required to be his assistant. What he didn't understand was that I had a project of my own that was just a little more important than a stinking garage. We were finally finished, and I raced in to shower and get dressed. I even borrowed a little cologne from Dad's bathroom. Wasn't sure how much to put on, so I just poured some in my hand and rubbed it on my neck. Then I wiped my hands on my shirt.

"Oh my gosh, you stink!" complimented my sister.

"Get lost, pipsqueak," I said, narrowing my eyes at her.

"Aaron, honey, I am choking. Did you pour the cologne bottle on your clothes?" Mom had come into the kitchen and was holding her hand over her face.

"Did I use too much?" I asked.

"You could say that. Better go wash off wherever you put it on. Maybe change your clothes if you put any there. You'll give people a headache." She fanned the newspaper in front of her face.

Well, how was I supposed to know how much to use? I raced back to my room, aware that it was already ten minutes until two. We would never make it. I scrubbed my neck with a washcloth and threw my shirt on the floor. I couldn't find another shirt I wanted to wear. They were all totally dorky. Finally I grabbed one that didn't look too much like a fifth-grade shirt and tried my kitchen entrance again.

"Well, is this better?"

"Nope, you still stink," Sarah said, laughing. She thought this was extremely funny and kept laughing and snorting until I hit her in the head with the newspaper.

"Yes, Aaron, I don't think you will hurt anyone's sinuses now. Stop hitting your sister."

We got in the car and Mom noticed we were low on gas. Dad had used her car and never filled it up.

"*Please* don't tell me we have to stop for gas, Mom. I'm late!" I'm sure my eyes were bugging out.

"We have to stop for gas, Aaron. I'm sorry, but I'm sure your friends won't run off and leave you. Do you have a meeting place?" Mom took a detour to the gas station.

"Yes. Please, please, please hurry."

"I won't take the time to fill it up, but if we don't stop, we won't make it at all." She hummed to the radio as she drove, totally unaware of the importance of that day.

I watched out the window as she moved, almost in slow motion, sliding the card into the gas pump, punching in some numbers or something, opening the little gas tank door, putting in the nozzle, and at long last, pumping gas! I stared out the window at her, trying to look as pitiful as possible. I tapped on the glass so she could get the full effect of my pitiful face. She just rolled her eyes at me.

It was eighteen minutes after two before we pulled up at the mall entrance. I leaped out of the car with Mom yelling, "Be careful, and call me when you're ready to come home!"

I waved and nodded to her as I ran into the mall and to the nearest escalator. I couldn't run up the escalator steps because some lady with a baby stroller and about eight kids was blocking my way. Why does time stand still whenever you're in a hurry?

Chapter 16

Cookie Intercepted

I could see the giant chocolate chip cookie hanging above the LLSGC store. I ran toward it, wondering if Kristin had given up and gone back home. There was such a huge crowd, I couldn't see if she was there.

As I got closer, I saw the back of her head. She wasn't alone. Another girl was with her and they were talking to ... oh no! Two guys. Kyle and some really big guy I didn't know.

I remembered Jessica telling me that Kristin liked Kyle. But maybe that had been a lie too.

I took a deep breath and tapped Kristin on the shoulder, expecting her to turn around and say, "There you are! I've been waiting for you."

But she just turned around and said, "Oh, hi, Aaron! What are you doing here?"

Huh? Had she not gotten my letter? Then why was she here, at the designated spot at the right time on the right day? Too weird. My head was all fuzzy. And who was this big guy, and why was Kristin already eating the perfect cookie, enjoying it without me?

"Hey, hey Haber-MAN, how's it going? Have you met Brock?" asked Kyle. "This is Aaron Haberman."

"No. Hi, Brock," I said, not really looking at him.

"He's already at Washburn Middle School. Seventh grader. Quarterback on the junior varsity football team," announced Kyle proudly. Kyle was always glad to hang with older, popular kids, especially athletes.

Great. A quarterback. So this guy was big *and* fast *and* probably not totally stupid. And he was reaching out to shake my hand.

"Nice to meet you, Aaron," said the giant kid as he applied a superhuman grip to my mere sixth-grade hand.

I gritted my teeth and hoped the bones in my hand would not be crushed. What did this guy do? Squeeze car tires in his spare time?

"Well, see you guys," said Big Brock. With a smile to Kristin, he said, "Looking forward to that dance, Kristin. Don't miss it!" He hugged her. Good grief, he actually hugged her.

Then he and Kyle left, probably looking for some other sixth graders to impress.

Kristin and the girl waved bye to them and then turned around to face me, giggling the way girls do. I did not have a clue what was going on.

"What dance?" I asked.

"Remember, the Get Acquainted Dance? In two weeks at the middle school? Brock is on the Planning and Greeting Committee.

Have you met my friend Laurie? She goes to Shaw Elementary and will be going to Washburn with us next year."

"Hi, Laurie," I said, barely looking at her. Brock had asked Kristin to a dance? This was too wild, too impossible. None of this was going according to my plan. Who was this mystery man, and how long had Kristin been crazy about him?

"So, Kristin, who do you think sent the note?" Laurie asked.

"Well, I don't know, but it's sort of exciting." Kristin looked a little pink and may actually have been blushing. She and I blushed more than any people I knew.

"Note?" I asked, hoping I sounded casual. My heart was thumping. Boy, did I need a cookie, but I figured I would choke on it at the moment.

"Yeah, Aaron, it was so strange. My sister found a note on our tree and brought it to me. I couldn't tell who it was from because when she tore it off the tree, the bottom part of the note was ripped off."

Bad, bad plan, Aaron. Way to go, Mr. Brilliance. Mr. Romance. What a loser I turned out to be. I could see it now. *"Brock and Kristin 'n' Love Forever" is carved on her front tree. And he hadn't even left the stinking note. I run into them and their three children at this very mall. He is a famous professional ball player, and she adores him and can't even recall who I am. Aaron Haberman? Is that the name of that kid who wore the huge cowboy boots to elementary school?*

"Wow, Kristin. That's really bizarre-a-mundo. Note in a tree. Well, I guess I'll go get a cookie."

Kristin finished her last bite and said, "Yeah, the cookies here are fantastic, Aaron. You'll love them. Guess we're gonna shop a little before my mom picks us up. See ya later. Bye." She flashed me a really sweet smile.

My cookie plan had been totally intercepted. It figures that it would have been by a football player.

Chapter 17

Chicken Dance

The Great Annual Sixth-Grade-Get-a-Look-at-This-New-Big-School-You-Will-Go-to-Next-Year Dance was in two days. I still hadn't decided if I would be going. Dancing was not a skill of mine. I could dance better than I could skate, but that wasn't saying much. And now I had to compete with Giant Older Cool Football Player Guy. He could probably dance too.

I went to the best dance source, Chris. "You gotta help me, dude. I need to learn to dance." Chris was so smooth, so good, I figured if he could just show me a few things, I could get by without looking like a sick chicken on the dance floor. That is, if I had to ask Kristin to dance in some kind of dance showdown at the OK Gym.

"When?" Chris asked. We were walking home from school together.

"Now," I said.

Chris stopped on the sidewalk, dropped his backpack, and said, "Okay, do this." He started humming and doing drum effects with his mouth and moving in ways I didn't think I could ever do.

I started laughing and said, "Not right now, dingnoid!"

He grinned and retrieved his stuff from the sidewalk. "Whatever."

At my house I threw my backpack in the door and told Mom I would be home after I visited Chris for a while. At his house we had access to good music and a little privacy. I was going to give it my best shot.

Chris locked his door and turned on his stereo. His mother wasn't home from work yet, so we cranked it up pretty loud. I have to give it to him. He wasn't a bad teacher, and we laughed as much as we did anything else. After about an hour, I had finished a basic tutorial on Dance Survival.

"You aren't so bad, Aaron," Chris said. "Keep practicing. Just listen to the music and loosen up. It doesn't matter that much what you do. Just *don't* do that thing where you bob your head up and down, and you might make it."

"Do I look like a chicken?" I asked.

He nodded and said, "You do look like a chicken with a broken neck when you do that head thing. So skip that move, man."

We high-fived each other and I headed home to do homework and dinner. I lay in bed wondering what was up with Kristin. She continued to be friendly at school, but for all I knew she was thinking of Big Brock and the Big Dance. This development was just a rotten piece of luck. And I felt like the moment was coming when I had to tighten my guts and speak up. All this confusion was confusing even me. I was tired of being such a wimp.

* * * * * * * * * *

The closer the dance got, the more nervous I became. I wasn't the only one.

"Aaron, are you going to the dance tonight?" Phil asked. "I don't know if I will. I mean, what are you supposed to do at a dance? Do you have to dance? *With* someone?"

Heavy sigh. "Yes, I am going, Phil. Even if it kills me."

"Why would it kill you?"

"Because I may have to go one-on-one with a real gladiator type."

"You mean fight?" Phil looked shocked.

"No, I mean I may have to ask someone to dance."

"The gladiator?" Phil's face was unbelieving.

"No ... worse. A girl."

Chapter 18

The Tiger Purrs

The Washburn Middle School gym was decorated with purple and yellow balloons. They were the school colors, I guess. Pretty ugly, if you ask me. There was a row of chairs at the front of the gym and lots of crepe paper streamers. The music was pretty good and pretty loud, but most kids were just standing around looking uncomfortable when Phil and I got there.

We went up to a group of guys we knew and started messing around, since no one had any clue what we were supposed to be doing. We got some punch, which was terrible, and a handful of chips. I hadn't seen Kristin yet, but Jessica came in, followed by Alicia Brown and Larry Shumberg. I began to wonder if they liked each other, or if they were just accidentally thrown together all the time. Alicia and Larry. What a pair they made. Maybe they would bother only each other if they hung out and leave the rest of us alone.

A very round woman walked up and tapped on the microphone, making that annoying sound over and over until it was obvious that, yes, the microphone *was* on. "Students! Students! Please gather at the front of the gym. We have some announcements to make."

Everyone reluctantly wandered toward the teacher and huddled in disinterested groups. We only wished for more music, better food, a few laughs, and a quick exit. I, of course, also wished for a moment with Kristin. And for Big Brock to move to Ireland or Brazil.

"We at Washburn Middle School want to welcome the next seventh-grade class! In just a few short months, you will all become part of the Washburn family!" Some cheerleaders ran out when she said this and jumped and yelled and threw pompoms around.

Some of us clapped, not really sure if that was expected. I wished I could feel more excited about becoming part of the Washburn family, but my mind wasn't really on this. I kept trying to turn around and look for Kristin.

"And now we would like to introduce some of our current seventh-grade student leaders, who will tell you a little about life at Washburn," the teacher proudly announced. There was scattered applause again. "Could someone turn the music down?" she asked. The applause stopped immediately.

Out walked an assortment of middle-school kids, some goofy looking, but most cute and probably popular. And, of course, the athletes, led by none other than Big Man on Campus, Brock-Man. I did not really listen to what was being said, but after four students stepped forward to tell us how Washburn was so much fun and such a cool place, suddenly one of the girls said, "So have fun tonight and we'll see ya soon." And the music came back on, louder than ever.

Those of us just barely still in elementary school and soon-to-be "big middle-school kids" quickly divided into four major groups: the food table group, the girl group, the guy group, and a few brave souls who stood on the edge of the dance floor. They weren't really dancing, just pretending to dance in little bursts and with no one in particular.

I saw Kristin with two girls, way over in the girl group. Phil and I were in the food table group, since someone had provided Hot Nacho chips and a giant bowl of candy. I saw Chris and another guy hook up with three girls and begin dancing a little farther out onto the actual dance floor. They were in a big group, all dancing at the same time. Everyone was watching. Some people clapped, appreciating the bravery of the new dance group and the smooth moves they were executing. A few other kids walked out there with them. Some tried to dance and others just goofed around. When the third fast song in a row started, I saw something that made my blood feel cold inside my arms and legs.

Brock, in a shirt with the popular wrestling character Boulder boldly on the front, started walking toward the girl group. It figured that "the Boulder" would be "the Brock's" hero. The way they both had more muscles than they could possibly use.

I stood, frozen, as I watched Brock walk up to Kristin and give her a little hug. There was no doubt this had become the worst day of my life. Then he started tugging on her arm, trying to drag her out onto the dance floor. She was laughing and trying to say no. How could she tell Brock she didn't want to dance? She had to go, of course. She was defenseless. I had to save her.

I started walking toward them, with Phil asking, "Hey, Aaron, where are you going?" I never even answered him. I was a man on a mission. Hoping it wouldn't be an impossible one. As I crossed the floor, I knew what I had to do. *I tap Brock on the shoulder and say, "Excuse me, but I believe the lady said she didn't want to dance. Unhand her." And Brock scrunches up his face and says, "I don't think so." I throw a punch at him before he even knows what's coming, and this big tree of a guy falls. And falls hard. Kristin grabs my hand, looks into my eyes, and says, "You saved me, Aaron. I kept hoping you would show up."*

By the time I got close, they were dancing after all. She didn't look too scared or mad. She was laughing, in fact, but that could be a cover. She was a brave girl and maybe a good actress.

I brushed past Kyle, who was now out dancing with some seventh-grade girl who had been up on the stage. I didn't know how he managed to do it. It was like he had magic vibes or something.

I stood just behind Brock, so, of course, Kristin couldn't see me. I was reaching up to tap him on the shoulder when Jessica grabbed my arm.

"Aaron, dance with me real quick. I need to ask you something," she said, looking a little nervous. As I turned around, she asked, "Hey, you're not still mad at me, are you?"

"Jessica, I'm a little busy right now."

"Aaron, *please*, I know I shouldn't ask after what I did to you, but I really need your help."

"With what, Jessica, making plans to ruin someone else's life?"

"Come on, Aaron, lighten up. It wasn't *that* bad," she insisted.

"Oh really? Could have fooled me. What's your big problem?" I asked.

"I really like someone and I need some advice."

"Oh, this is rich, Jessica. You must be crazy."

"Well, I don't have anyone else to ask. You're his good friend. I want to know about him and if he likes me." She looked at me with that begging eye look, like the one you give your mother when she takes the fresh cookies out of the oven.

She probably likes Kyle, I thought, *like every other girl does, I guess.* "Fine, so what do you want to know about Kyle?" I asked.

"Kyle? Nothing! He's a show-off. I want to know about Phil!" Jessica said.

You could have knocked me over with a pencil. This was absolutely the last person I thought she would ask about. "I don't believe you, Jessica," I said.

We still weren't dancing, just standing in the middle of the dance floor with several couples dancing around us, but most of them were talking more than dancing.

"He's so sweet and quiet. I'm not kidding, Aaron."

"Well, sure, Jess. I'll be happy to tell you all about Phil. Let's see, he likes sushi. Ya know … raw, dead fish? He loves Japanese movies, in Japanese, and if you really want to impress him, you'll learn to sky-dive." I grinned a real phony grin.

"Very funny, Aaron. Just tell me, does he like anyone?"

"Jessica, Phil mainly likes his dog and his video games," I said, shaking my head at the idea of Jessica and Phil. But who knew? Anything could happen, I guess.

I turned away from Jessica in time to see Brock and Kristin start to leave the dance floor. I walked as fast as I could, fear causing my heart to thud so loud, I could hear it in my ears. Please, I silently asked, please don't let me get smeared in front of Kristin.

"Brock!" I said. The music drowned me out. He didn't even turn around.

"*Brock!*" I said, louder. Oh, my gosh, he turned around. Was I crazy or what?

"Hey! How's it going? Aaron, isn't it?" Brock smiled. "What do you think of Washburn so far?"

Ha! His tactics to get me off track wouldn't work as easily as that!

"I want …," my voice cracked. Perfect. "I want to … dance with Kristin," I said. *The room seems to freeze. Only the roar of applause from everyone in the room can be heard as I push Brock out of the way and step around him to claim Kristin. "We're out of here, babe," I say as the credits roll in the award-winning movie of our life.*

No roar. No applause. Just Brock saying, "Sure. You guys have fun."

Huh? No battle? I had finally stepped up, ready to fight for what I wanted. Would it be this easy? Was it a trick?

Brock walked off, waving, and Kristin smiled at me. She

might have been blushing, but there wasn't too much light in the gym, so I couldn't tell.

"I was hoping you'd show up," Kristin said.

That was what she had said in my daydream. My real world and my fantasy world had accidentally collided, like in some space movie. I realized today was my new best day, for sure.

Now I was blushing. I knew it because I felt my face get hot, like it did when I mowed the yard too fast. I hoped she wouldn't be able to see it.

"You want to dance?" I asked.

"Well, we could. Or we could eat something. You saw that they have Hot Nacho chips and a big bowl of candy," she said, smiling.

See, I had always known this was the girl of my dreams.

"What about Brock? Will he be mad?" I asked as we walked over to the food table.

"What do you mean?" Kristin wrinkled her face at me.

"Well, you know, if you guys are … going out or whatever," I said.

Kristin had just taken a big bite of a chip, and now she laughed so hard and fast that some of the chip flew out of her mouth.

"Aaron, Brock is … my cousin. You thought we were …? No way. He's always been like a big brother to me."

We looked at each other and both started laughing. We didn't say anything else for a while, just hung out together and consumed a lot of food.

We looked out on the dance floor, watching Chris still dancing with three girls and looking really great. Larry Shumberg was doing some version of the old robot dance. Alicia was clapping and everyone else was rolling their eyes. Larry had a lot of guts to get out there and look like a moron, I guess.

"So, Kristin," I said, feeling I might be able to talk to her like we were actually from the same planet. I felt nervous, but not sick-nervous. "I need to tell you something."

"Okay, Aaron. What?"

"You know that note on your tree?" I asked, trying to make myself look at her and not at the floor.

"Yeah?" Kristin had a strange look on her face. Like she didn't know if some creature was about to jump out at her.

"It was me. It was me who wrote it. I didn't think about the limb going through the note or tearing off part of it or that anything like that could happen. I'm sorry. I didn't mean to freak you out." I tried to look like I was sorry and hoped she had a good sense of humor, or would at least feel sorry for me.

"Oh, no, Aaron, the note didn't freak me out. I sort of ... thought it might be from you. But then there wasn't a name on it anymore, so I didn't really know."

"Uh, Kristin ... are you freaked that the note *is* from me?" Now I looked like *I* might be expecting that creature to jump out.

"No," she said, laughing and shaking her head. "And while we're being honest, I guess I should tell you that I almost wrote you the same kind of note, but I chickened out."

Wow, I couldn't believe it. I had never even needed a secret operation. It was like we were two tigers in the same jungle, tracking each other at the same time.

"So Aaron, do you think it's weird that I almost wrote you?"

"No way," I answered, beaming. "You want to come over sometime and shoot some baskets? Or is that just a guy thing?"

"A guy thing?" she asked, grinning. "Let's see what the final score is and we'll see if it's a guy thing or not." When she smiled, I got to see those crinkling gray eyes right up close.

It's really true that you can never tell what's going to happen. And that the worst day of your life and the best day of your life can be the same day.

The End

G. L. Eaves